The Rewindable Clock

by Aaron Starmer
illustrated by Courtney La Forest

Penguin Workshop

To Gwenn and Jim—AS

For my dear Grammy—thank you for always
believing in me and encouraging me to
work hard. I love you to Pluto and back—CLF

PENGUIN WORKSHOP
An Imprint of Penguin Random House LLC, New York

Penguin supports copyright. Copyright fuels creativity, encourages diverse voices,
promotes free speech, and creates a vibrant culture. Thank you for buying an authorized
edition of this book and for complying with copyright laws by not reproducing, scanning,
or distributing any part of it in any form without permission. You are supporting writers
and allowing Penguin to continue to publish books for every reader.

The publisher does not have any control over and does not assume any
responsibility for author or third-party websites or their content.

Text copyright © 2020 by Aaron Starmer. Illustrations copyright © 2020 by
Penguin Random House LLC. All rights reserved. Published by Penguin Workshop, an
imprint of Penguin Random House LLC, New York. PENGUIN and PENGUIN WORKSHOP
are trademarks of Penguin Books Ltd, and the W colophon is a registered trademark of
Penguin Random House LLC. Manufactured in China.

Visit us online at www.penguinrandomhouse.com.

Library of Congress Cataloging-in-Publication Data is available upon request.

ISBN 9780593222867 (pbk)   10 9 8 7 6 5 4 3 2 1
ISBN 9780593094303 (hc)   10 9 8 7 6 5 4 3 2 1

Chapter One

LATE

Keisha James was late for the bus.

How late? One minute late, which was a big, big deal.

Not that she missed the bus. Oh no, she would never do that. But she usually arrived at the bus stop at 7:05 a.m. Today she arrived at 7:06 a.m. And even though the bus wouldn't pull up until 7:08 a.m., this was clearly disastrous.

Why? Because it meant she was sixth

in line. If she had arrived one minute earlier, she would've been third in line, which is clearly better. You see, Keisha's bus stop was the last one on the route to Hopewell Elementary. By the time the bus pulled up, seats were always hard to come by. If she was at least third in line, she'd get a decent seat, somewhere in the middle, maybe next to Devon Garcia or Kendall Ali.

But sixth in line? It meant sitting in—avert your eyes if you're the sensitive type—a hump seat!

Oh, the dreaded hump seats, the most vile and wretched of all seats on the bus. Located directly above the back wheels, the hump seats were impossibly uncomfortable because anyone who sat in them couldn't fully extend their legs or put their backpack on the bus floor. So they had to sit with their backpacks in their laps, pushed against their chests by their bent knees.

In other words, sixth in line was bad. Very bad. And today it was even worse. Today it meant sitting in the hump seat next to Hunter Barnes.

No one at Hopewell Elementary wanted to sit in *any* seat next to Hunter Barnes.

Sadly for Keisha, it was the only option. No students were sick. The bus was as full as it could be. So she reluctantly accepted her fate, trudging to the back and asking Hunter, "May I please sit here?"

Hunter's backpack was in the way, and he grumbled under his breath as he moved it to his lap. "Whatever."

This was Hunter being as polite as he could possibly be. Because there's no other way to put it: Hunter Barnes was a bully.

Not the kind of bully who would beat kids up. Worse. The kind who would figure out how to make their lives miserable with nothing but words.

For instance, a kid named Carson Cooper once wore a red shirt to school, and Hunter told him, "People who wear red shirts smell like wet socks filled with dog food and boiled cauliflower. But people who wear blue shirts smell like chocolate chip cookies."

Hunter was, of course, wearing a blue shirt when he said this.

So the next day, Carson was sure to

use extra soap in the shower. And he put on his best blue shirt and stood for an hour next to an oven that was baking chocolate chip cookies. Then he set off to school confident in his shirt choice and smell.

But then Hunter, of course, showed up to school wearing a red shirt.

"Eww, why are you wearing a blue shirt?" he asked Carson. "Everyone knows people in blue shirts smell like dirty diapers filled with tuna fish sandwiches."

Hunter did this sort of thing to almost every kid at Hopewell Elementary. Except, that is, to Keisha.

Because Keisha was focused. Keisha was fierce. Keisha did not suffer fools.

Which means she didn't tolerate any sort of nonsense, especially from kids like Hunter.

That morning on the bus, she was ready. If he said anything to insult or tease her, she was armed with a comeback that would absolutely destroy him.

Obviously, she wasn't going to use that comeback unless she was provoked. Above all, Keisha believed in honesty and integrity. And even though Hunter didn't know what Keisha had in store for him, he was smart enough to know that she always came to school prepared. The temptation to tease her was strong, but he resisted. It wasn't worth the risk of finding out how devastating one of her comebacks could be.

So the two sat together silently in that godforsaken hump seat, with their knees pushing their backpacks against their chests, and their eyes pointed straight ahead.

It was a bad way for both of them to start the day.

Chapter Two

HOMEROOM

The day could get worse.

And the day would get worse.

But before it got worse, it wasn't too bad.

Keisha hurried off the bus and directly to homeroom.

As always, she was the first person to arrive. *Person* is the important word here. Because two goldfish were already in the room. They were always in the room.

Finn and Gill were their names, and they lived in a bowl on a table next to the radiator. They were the classroom mascots, and the kids all loved them. But Keisha was the one responsible for feeding them.

Why? Because everyone else was lazy. Or at least that's what Keisha thought. She had nominated herself for the job at the beginning of the school year, when she assumed no one else was responsible enough to do it.

"I don't know how you two would

survive without me," she said as she sprinkled their flaky food onto the water. "Maybe someday you'll thank me."

"In the meantime, perhaps my gratitude will be enough," a voice answered.

It wasn't the fish talking. It was Keisha's homeroom teacher, Mrs. Shen. She was setting her bag on her desk in preparation for another day. In many kids' minds, Mrs. Shen was Hopewell Elementary's best teacher. She was certainly one of the friendliest. And she always gave Keisha an enthusiastic greeting.

"So thank you, Keisha," Mrs. Shen said. "And a good morning to you."

Keisha turned around and replied,

"Correction, Mrs. Shen. *A great* morning. Great."

"What makes this morning so great?" Mrs. Shen asked.

"Potential," Keisha said. "Every day has the potential to be the best day of my life. And if I work harder than the day before, there's a good chance it will be."

"I like that attitude," Mrs. Shen said. "Very much."

Keisha wasn't exaggerating. She tried to make every day a better day than the previous one. It didn't always happen. And sometimes she regretted her decisions.

Maybe I should've talked to Hunter on the bus, she thought as Hunter waltzed into the room. He sat down in a corner in the back, far away from anyone else.

Bullies only want attention, she thought. *What if I gave him good attention? Maybe he wouldn't be so mean to everyone.*

But the past was in the past, and there was nothing she could do to change it.

She would have to try harder tomorrow.

Chapter Three
OH NO

Keisha's first class of the day was music with Mr. Gregson. Mr. Gregson was a quiet guy with a ponytail and thick-rimmed glasses. He played bass guitar in a band called the Screamin' Beagles.

Keisha had seen the Screamin' Beagles perform at a local restaurant once. Sadly, there were no beagles in the lineup, and there was absolutely no screamin'. Unless

you count slightly off-key singing as screamin'.

The Screamin' Beagles performed mostly covers of songs that were around when Keisha's parents were kids.

It was hard to say if they were good at it, because Keisha didn't listen to that type of music. And it always made her a bit uneasy to see a teacher outside of school.

She preferred to see her teachers standing at the front of a classroom, telling kids what to do. Teaching, in other words, like Mr. Gregson was doing now.

"Today we will be practicing for the concert," Mr. Gregson told the class. "So everyone take their places, and we'll start learning the lyrics to one of my favorite songs, 'Time After Time.'"

"I looove this song," Bryce Dodd whispered to Keisha as they lined up on the room's makeshift stage.

Bryce was a weird, but nice, kid. So Keisha assumed this would be a weird, but nice, song.

"I don't know if I've ever heard of 'Time After Time,'" Keisha said.

Bryce replied, "The Screamin' Beagles

do an amazing version. I was actually listening to their recording of it last night when I was doing my science homework and—"

Keisha didn't hear anything else, because the words *science homework* had nearly knocked her unconscious.

Oh.

No.

She remembered Mrs. Shen assigning science homework.

She remembered slipping science homework into her homework folder.

But she did not remember *doing* her science homework.

Oh.

No.

This was not like Keisha at all. She

had never forgotten to do her homework.
Ever.

She raised her hand.

"Yes, Keisha?" Mr. Gregson said.

"May I please be excused?"

"May I ask why?"

"Because I honestly might faint.
Right here, right now, face-first into the
bongos."

It wasn't a lie. And Mr. Gregson could
tell by the queasy look in Keisha's eyes.
He handed her a hall pass and said, "Go."

Keisha went. Only she didn't go to the
bathroom or the nurse's office.

She went to Locker 37.

Chapter Four

LOCKER 37

Now let's get a few things out of the way.

Hopewell Elementary was an elementary school, obviously.

It had teachers who taught students from kindergarten to fourth grade, as most elementary schools do.

On its second floor, there was a faulty drinking fountain that dribbled water, so kids had to put their mouths on the nozzle, which was super gross.

In the kitchen of its cafetorium sat something called a convection oven, which was basically like a regular oven, only it "convected" food. Or something like that. The only thing you really need to know about it is that it cooked food quickly. It was a very exciting type of oven, at least to people who care about ovens.

Oh yeah, and Hopewell Elementary was home to Locker 37.

You know about Locker 37, don't you?

The greatest locker that ever was or ever shall be?

Quite possibly the most amazing, incredible, jaw-droppingly magnificent collection of atoms in the known universe?

Ring any bells?

Don't worry. Even if you don't know about Locker 37, Keisha did.

On the first day of fourth grade, Keisha's classmate Carson Cooper found a note written by the previous fourth-grade class. It was all about Locker 37. One part of the note said:

If you or another fourth-grader has a problem (any problem!), open Locker 37 and the locker will provide a solution. It won't always be the solution you want, or expect, but it is guaranteed to work.

Word got around that Locker 37 had been casting its magic for years. But only for fourth-graders. Once a kid moved on to fifth grade, they forgot about it. And younger kids weren't allowed to know about it.

Which was fine by Keisha. She didn't want anyone else to figure out what she was up to. All she wanted to do was open Locker 37, pull out some finished homework, and go on with her day.

But things are never that simple, are they?

Chapter Five

THE REWINDABLE CLOCK

Inside the glorious glowing belly of Locker 37, Keisha found . . . a clock.

Not a phone with the time on the screen, or even a watch. There was no digital display or wristband on it. It was a genuine old-school clock. Which means it was a small round device with

gears on the inside, a glass face on the

outside, and twelve numbers and three

rotating hands beneath the glass. If you

knew how to read it, you could tell the time of day.

Keisha did know how to read it, but she'd never seen such a small clock before. It fit in the palm of her hand.

"This is not what I wanted, you, you, you . . . *locker*!" she hollered.

"It never is," a voice replied.

Keisha turned to find Carson Cooper behind her.

"What are you doing here?" she asked.

"I was sorta hoping to use Locker 37," Carson said. "But I guess you beat me to it."

Carson moved his left elbow across

his chest and turned away.

"Another stain?" Keisha asked.

Carson sighed and nodded. When it came to getting stains on clothes, Carson was a seasoned pro. He had once even managed to get both a wasabi and a Vegemite stain on the toe of his sock. It was an impressive feat on its own, but even more impressive when you consider that Carson didn't know what those things were.

Keisha held up the clock and told him, "Not sure if this will help you, but it sure isn't helping me. I already know what time it is."

"What do you need help with?" Carson asked.

"I'd rather not say."

"It's embarrassing?"

"Extremely."

That might seem like an exaggeration. But for Keisha, it wasn't. She was the best student in fourth grade. All the other students were in awe of her commitment to excellence. So forgetting to do her homework was beyond embarrassing. She might as well have been running through the gym in nothing but her underwear.

"I once ran through the gym in nothing but my underwear," Carson told Keisha. "I survived it. Whatever you're facing can't be as bad as that."

"Speak for yourself," Keisha said as she ran her fingers over the surface of the clock.

It was smooth and didn't have any buttons on it. There was a knob on the top, however. And when she flipped it over, she found a message etched in the back:

TO WIND THE CLOCK,
PULL THE KNOB AND TURN

Carson could've told her that Locker 37 didn't give out the most detailed instructions, because he knew more about Locker 37 than anyone else in the fourth grade. After all, he was the first one in their class to use it. When he used the locker, he found an eraser inside that would erase . . . well, anything. But all that was written on the eraser was *Rub Three Times*.

"Lemme guess," Carson said. "That clock stops time."

"Who knows?" Keisha said. "Let's see."

She did what the words said. She pulled the knob out from the clock about a quarter of an inch.

There was a *click!*

The second hand stopped moving.

She tried to turn the knob clockwise to wind it. But it didn't budge.

So she turned the knob counter-clockwise. The minute hand moved backward a little bit, and then stopped.

The time on the clock had been the correct time: 8:19.

But it was now set to 8:16.

"Did anything happen?" Carson asked.

Keisha looked around. "Nope."

This was true. *Nothing* had happened. Yet.

"Maybe it's a dud," Carson said.

"I guess so," Keisha replied.

Then she pushed the knob back in.

Click.

The second hand started moving again.

And that's when *everything* happened.

Chapter Six

8:16

Perhaps saying that *everything* happened is a bit of an exaggeration. Exactly one very, very big thing happened.

Keisha became confused. Keisha was rarely confused.

You see, Carson had moved. Instantly. He had been standing right next to her, and then—*poof!*—he was suddenly at the end of the hall.

"How did you get all the way over there?" Keisha asked.

"I walked," Carson replied as he paced toward her.

"But you were standing right next to me," she said.

"No, I just got here," he replied. "I was sorta hoping to use Locker 37. But I guess you beat me to it."

Then Carson moved his left elbow across his chest, covering the stain on his shirt, and he turned away.

Keisha checked the clock. The second hand was ticking.

The time read 8:16, which was the exact time she had opened Locker 37.

"Oh," she said. "You didn't say the same thing to me a few minutes ago, did you?"

Carson shook his head. "I haven't talked to you at all today."

"Oh," Keisha said again. And she checked the clock once more.

It was now 8:17.

She pulled the knob out—*click*—and turned it until it stopped at 8:16. She pushed it back in—*click*—and Carson was suddenly at the end of the hall again.

"How did you get all the way over there?" Keisha asked.

"I walked," Carson said as he paced toward her.

"But you were standing right next to me a second ago."

"No, I just got here. I was sorta hoping to use Locker 37. But I guess you beat me to it."

Carson used the exact same words, for the third time in a row.

And wouldn't you know it, he moved his left elbow across his chest, covering the stain on his shirt, and he turned away. Exactly like he had done twice before.

Either she was having a serious case of déjà vu or . . .

The clock was a time machine!

Chapter Seven
TESTING 1, 2, 3

Keisha tested the clock a few more times to make sure she was correct. Each time, she would talk to Carson for a few minutes, and then she'd pull the knob out—*click*—and turn it until it stopped at 8:16, and then she'd push the knob back in—*click*.

Poof! Carson would be back at the end of the hall with no memory of their conversation. Of course, Keisha remembered everything.

The conclusion was obvious. She was traveling back in time. And she had already figured out the rules.

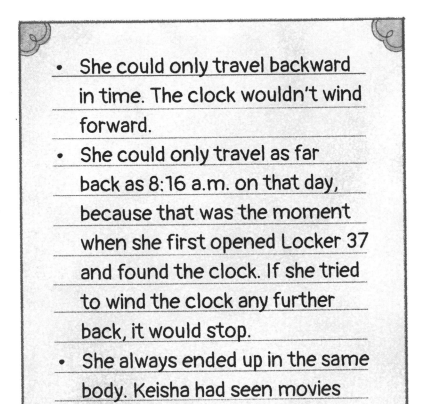

- She could only travel backward in time. The clock wouldn't wind forward.
- She could only travel as far back as 8:16 a.m. on that day, because that was the moment when she first opened Locker 37 and found the clock. If she tried to wind the clock any further back, it would stop.
- She always ended up in the same body. Keisha had seen movies

where time travelers would
bump into younger versions
of themselves. Fortunately,
that wasn't happening here.
There weren't multiple Keishas
running around the school. It
was her mind that was traveling
back in time, not her body.

- Finally, she was the only one
who could use it. This was
actually Keisha's own rule. She
wasn't about to give the power
of time travel to some other
kid who might commit acts
of mischief and mayhem. Talk
about irresponsible!

Now that she knew the rules, she had to figure out how to get her homework done. Traveling back in time a few minutes in the same hallway so she could have the same conversation with Carson Cooper didn't seem like the best strategy.

So she started over once more, only now she simply grabbed the clock and hurried past Carson without saying a word.

It was time to get to work.

Chapter Eight

THE PROBLEM WITH TIME TRAVEL

Time travel is a tricky thing. It's extremely vulnerable to paradoxes. If you don't know what a paradox is, here's a famous example: A guy builds a time machine. That guy uses the time machine to go back in time and make sure his parents never meet each other.

There are a couple of problems with this scenario.

Number one:

The guy is a real creep. Seriously. Doesn't he want his parents to find love?

Number two:

The guy isn't very smart. If his parents never meet, then he will never be born.

If he will never be born, then he will never make a time machine.

Which means he will never go back in time and stop his parents from meeting.

Which means his parents will fall in

love, and he will be born.

Which means he will make a time machine and go back in time and make sure his parents never meet.

If his parents never meet, then he will never be born and —

Let's take a breather.

Because you could continue with this sort of reasoning for an infinite amount of time, or until the universe collapses, though that's hardly recommended. Instead, consider an alternative, something that's essentially the video-game version of time travel.

What if every time a person traveled back in time, they started a new timeline, like starting over, or from a particular save point, in a video game?

Each time someone restarts a video game, it branches off into a new timeline, right? That person will have the knowledge they've gained from each previous round of game play. And that knowledge will make them a better player. But the individual timelines created won't affect one another.

In other words, time travel is not one continual loop. It's a series of branches that will never meet.

So if our creep from the paradox

goes back and messes with his mom and dad, it won't matter. He will have hopped over to another timeline, started another round of a video game, created another branch in his story. This new past won't affect his old future.

Get it?

Of course you do, because you're brilliant.

And on the off chance that you don't get it, that's also okay. Even the very best time travelers often don't *get* it. They focus their energy on *doing* it.

Simply imagine that Keisha was in a video game, and she didn't have to

worry about the logic of time travel.
She could restart her game whenever
she wanted, at any point in the day
after she opened Locker 37. And she
had only one concern.

How was she going to win?

Chapter Nine
FINDING TIME

Keisha hurried back to music class.
As she pushed open the door,
Bryce waved to her.

Mr. Gregson was pointing to lyrics on
the whiteboard, which Keisha ducked
in front of as she crossed the room. She
slipped back onstage next to Bryce.

While Mr. Gregson's back was turned,
she whispered to Bryce, "How long did it
take you to do the science homework?"

Bryce considered the question for a moment, then said, "An hour, maybe."

That was a long time to be doing science homework, but Keisha knew Bryce had a wandering mind. So it was possible that he had spent half of that hour daydreaming about talking gummy bears.

Actually, it was more than possible. It was likely. Because the next thing Bryce whispered was "There's something that's been really bothering me lately."

"What's that?"

"If gummy bears could talk, what do you think they'd talk about?"

Keisha stared at him in disbelief. "I think they'd say you spend too much time doing homework."

"Really?"

"Yeah," Keisha said. "Because I bet I could do that science homework in less than thirty minutes."

"Wait," Bryce said, and this time he didn't whisper it. "You didn't do the science homework?"

"I didn't say that!"

"I think you did!"

And like that, Keisha was busted! But not only by Bryce.

Mr. Gregson cleared his throat, which was not a good sign. Mr. Gregson didn't yell. He hardly ever raised his voice. But if he cleared his throat . . . *oh boy*. It meant this mellow music teacher meant business.

"Miss James and Mr. Dodd," he said

slowly, "unless you are discussing the lyrics to the immortal classic 'Time After Time,' then I kindly ask you to shut . . . your . . . mouths. This is your reminder."

"But, Mr. Gregson, this is serious, it's about gummy bears and how—" Bryce started to say, but Mr. Gregson was not having it.

"And now *this* is your warning," he said. "You don't want to face the consequences, do you, Bryce? Keisha? You don't want me to send you to—"

Vice Principal Meehan's office.

That was what Mr. Gregson was about to say. But he never had the chance to say it.

Keisha didn't want Bryce to remember she had forgotten to do her homework.

And she certainly didn't want to be sent to Vice Principal Meehan's office for the first time in her life.

So she pulled out the knob on the clock—*click*—and she turned it back three minutes, to the moment before she reentered Mr. Gregson's class. She pushed the knob back in—*click!*

Poof! She was back in the hallway.

"Okay," she told herself. "I need to find thirty minutes to do my homework. No more mistakes."

As Keisha pushed open the classroom door, Bryce waved to her for the second time. And once again, Mr. Gregson was pointing to lyrics on the whiteboard, which she ducked in front of as she crossed the room.

Just like last time, she slipped back onstage next to Bryce. But she didn't say anything to him during this new timeline. There was no need to have that conversation again.

Chapter Ten

HOMEWORK SPRINT

Once music was over, Keisha ran to social studies. And she used the clock to time how long it took her.

Two minutes and thirty-three seconds. That left her with two minutes and

twenty-seven seconds of free time before
social studies started. Counting social
studies, she had seven more periods that
day, and some of the locations were closer
together than the music and social studies
rooms. Some were farther apart. So Keisha
figured she could have, on average, two
minutes and thirty seconds of free time
before each period. But that was only if she
ran from one location to the next.

Added up, it would give her a total
of close to twenty minutes for the day.

Was that enough time to do her science homework? Maybe, but everything had to go exactly her way.

She had to be as focused as she'd ever been.

She couldn't be distracted by other students or teachers.

And she had to make sure she didn't get in any trouble.

After all, running in the hall was against the rules, and she was lucky she wasn't caught the first time she did it. Her luck was sure to run out.

That is, unless she talked to Riley Zimmerman.

Ever since kindergarten, Riley Zimmerman had been the class's maestro of mischief. Her pranks were too numerous to count, but among her greatest were:

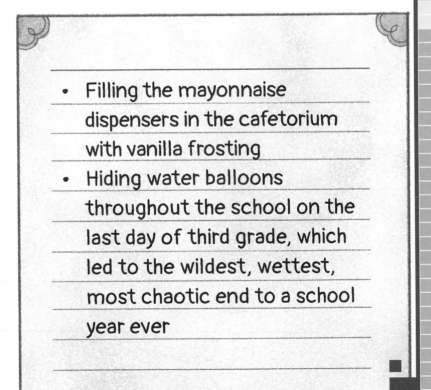

- Filling the mayonnaise dispensers in the cafetorium with vanilla frosting
- Hiding water balloons throughout the school on the last day of third grade, which led to the wildest, wettest, most chaotic end to a school year ever

- Convincing at least seven of her classmates that there was a pirate's treasure buried beneath the playground's sandbox and then watching in delight as they dug a four-foot-deep hole

The most astounding thing was that even with all of Riley's obvious shenanigans, she had never faced serious consequences. Keisha was pretty sure Riley had never even been sent to Vice Principal Meehan's office. She needed to know her secrets.

Sitting at her desk, waiting for social

studies to start, Keisha stared at a blank worksheet that was supposed to contain her science homework. When Riley stepped into the room, Keisha jumped to her feet and waved excitedly.

Riley approached her, and Keisha asked, "How's it going?"

"Not so good," Riley said. "Today is supposed to be fish stick day for lunch, but they're all out of fish sticks. So now it's cheesy breadstick day. Cheesy breadsticks are the food of pure evil."

Keisha couldn't sympathize. She, like every fourth-grader who wasn't Riley, would've always preferred cheesy breadstick day to fish stick day. Because cheesy breadsticks were delicious, and fish sticks were gross.

But she wasn't going to offend this
fish stick aficionado by telling her that.

"I wish I could help you," Keisha told
Riley instead. "But I'm in the middle of my
own *much* bigger problem right now."

"And what problem could possibly be

bigger than a school without fish sticks?"
Riley said with a gasp.

Keisha looked over both her shoulders
for witnesses, and when she didn't see
any, she leaned forward and whispered,
"I'll tell you . . . if you can teach me how to
be bad."

Chapter Eleven
CREATIVE TRUTHS

Riley's eyes lit up.

She put her hands together and wiggled her fingers in utter delight. "So you want to be bad, huh? Where to start, where to start . . ."

"I might as well start by telling you everything," Keisha said. "Since I'll just be going back in time right after we talk, and you won't remember a word of this conversation, anyway."

Riley's eyebrows arched. "You're going where, now?"

"A bit of harmless time travel," Keisha said. "Don't worry about it. All you need to know is that I forgot to do my science homework, and I'm trying to find time to do it during the day. So I'm running between classes, and I don't want to get in trouble. Please teach me how to be bad."

"Okay, correct me if I'm wrong," Riley said. "Your idea of being bad is . . . doing your homework?"

"Exactly," Keisha said. "Homework I *forgot* to do. It is possibly the worst thing that's ever happened to me."

Riley put a hand over her eyes

and shook her head. "Holy fettuccine Alfredo. I don't even know where to start with that. But if you need to do some homework, why don't you do it at lunch? What about recess?"

"Um, you're not allowed to do homework at lunch or recess," Keisha said. "The monitors watch you like hawks. Besides, even if I could get away with it, I'm not going to sacrifice my nourishment or social time, even for one day. They're almost as important as my intellectual pursuits."

"How old are you again?"

"Ten."

"And you use words like *intellectual pursuits*?"

"If you care about getting into a good

college, you should consider using words like that, too."

"I don't have to worry about that, since I've already been accepted into MIT," Riley said with a wink. "It's one of the best colleges in the country, in case you didn't know."

"What? You? But . . . ?"

"I'm kidding," Riley said. "Listen. If you're worried about getting busted for running in the hall, the solution is simple. Be prepared."

No one had to tell Keisha to be prepared. Preparation was in her bones. In her blood. Every cell of her body knew how important preparation was.

"What sort of preparation are we talking about here?" Keisha said. "Do you mean I should have smoke bombs or banana peels or, like, *Mario Kart*–type stuff to slow down any pursuers?"

Riley laughed. "That'd be awesome, but no. What you really need is excuses. You should be prepared to say you're having a bathroom emergency. Or that you're running from Hunter Barnes. Or that cockroaches are falling out of the sky."

"But those would be lies," Keisha said.

"I prefer to think of them as creative truths. I mean, all of those things are technically possible."

"I don't tell creative truths. I only tell truth truths."

"Then I don't know how to help you. Creative truths are my specialty."

"Maybe I should go back in time, and

we can have this conversation again, and you'll give me a better answer."

"Yeah, I meant to ask you about that time-travel stuff," Riley said. "How exactly are you going to pull that off?"

"I have a time machine," Keisha said, showing Riley the clock. "I'm going to use it a few seconds from now, and you won't know we ever had this conversation. But I'll remember everything."

"Well, if you have a time machine, can't you go back in time and try things over and over again? You know, so you don't ever get in trouble? Practice makes perfect, right?"

Riley was right, of course. And Keisha was embarrassed that she hadn't thought of it herself. But she wasn't going to give

Riley the satisfaction of knowing that.
She pulled the knob on the clock—*click*—
turned it back three minutes, and pushed
it back in—*click*.

Poof!

Keisha walked into social studies and
sat down. She set her backpack on her
desk, to block Mrs. Shen's view. With her
homework in her lap, she worked for
two minutes and twenty-seven seconds.
When Riley walked in, Keisha didn't even
look up.

Chapter Twelve

THE BEST ROUTE

After social studies, Keisha ran to language arts. This usually wouldn't require any running, because Mrs. Shen taught both classes, but today, of course, had to be different. Language arts was meeting in the library to preview the upcoming book fair, and Keisha was determined to arrive well before the other students. So off she ran. Unfortunately, as she bounded down a staircase, she came face-to-face with Vice Principal Meehan.

"Miss James!" Meehan exclaimed. "Of all the children I'd expect to see zipping down the stairs, you would be the last one!"

"Don't worry," Keisha said as she held the knob on the clock. "You never saw it."

Click. Turn. Click. Poof.

One minute back in time. Her run was reset.

Keisha bypassed that staircase this time and took another route far away from Meehan. But this route landed her in the sights of Mr. Trundle, the gym teacher.

"Young lady, save that energy for dodgeball tomorrow," he said. "Slow it down, or you're heading to consequence town."

There was a punishment system at Hopewell Elementary that was known as Reminder, Warning, Consequence.

It was essentially a three-strike rule. First you get a gentle reminder, then a stern warning, and finally a consequence, which could range from being asked to sit out an activity to being sent to the vice principal's office.

Of course, some teachers simply skipped the reminder or warning if the infraction was serious enough.

For instance, if a kid tackled a teacher, that kid would go right to the consequence phase. Not that any kid would ever tackle a teacher, of course.

Every fourth-grader at Hopewell Elementary had received a reminder at one point or another. Most had received warnings. More than half of them had faced consequences. But not Keisha. Never Keisha. And she was going to keep her streak alive.

Click. Turn. Click. Poof.

Once again, she went back a minute and avoided the route with Meehan, and the route with Trundle, choosing instead to cut through the cafetorium and hustle down the back hall. This route, while ten seconds longer, was the winner, and she

arrived at the library with three minutes
and six seconds to spare.

She used those precious minutes
and seconds to hide in the corner with
the picture books and do her science
homework.

Chapter Thirteen
ALMOST DONE

The rest of the day was hard work. Keisha tried and tried again until she got it all right.

Click. Turn. Click. Poof.

She ran and ran and ran some more.

Click. Turn. Click. Poof.

She received reminders and warnings from teachers, and she started over from the beginning, over and over again, trying to find as much time as humanly possible.

Click. Turn. Click. Poof.
Click. Turn. Click. Poof.
Click. Turn. Click. Poof.

Before long, she had nearly perfected each dash to class. She slid down banisters. She slipped out the front door, ran through the playground, hurdling seesaws and swings, and slipped back in the side door to avoid detection.

Click. Turn. Click. Poof.

As Keisha often reminded people, she was the president of the Junior Janitor Club. Which meant she had a set of the janitor's keys. The keys certainly came in handy, because now she could duck into janitor closets as teachers walked past. Then she could sneak back into the hall and keep running . . . running . . . running!

Click. Turn. Click. Poof.

She staged distractions, such as throwing handfuls of miniature bags of Skittles behind her and causing children to pile up like they were under a piñata.

Click. Turn. Click. Poof.

She didn't talk to anyone unless absolutely necessary.

Click. Turn. Click. Poof.

Yet she still managed to eat her lunch at a consistent pace, which helped her digestion. And to socialize at recess, which proved to her classmates that she could indeed be a likable character. And to raise her hand in each of her classes and to answer questions correctly each and every time, which helped remind everyone that there was nothing that Keisha wasn't good at.

Click. Turn. Click. Poof.

By the time she was at art, her second-to-last class of the day, she had cobbled together enough free time to finish her science homework.

The feeling was exhilarating, but exhausting. With all her time traveling, she had added an extra five hours to her day. A lot of that extra time was spent running. It was like being in a marathon. Thankfully, she could see the finish line.

Chapter Fourteen
OH NO, PART 2

When Bryce arrived at art class, Keisha waved her worksheet in his face.

"Done!" she said. "In less than twenty minutes. I even finished a class early!"

Bryce had no clue why she was bragging. In this particular timeline, they never had the conversation about homework. Of course, Keisha remembered that other timeline and conversation, but he sure didn't.

Bryce was polite, however, because he was always polite. "That's some good-looking homework you got there. When is it due?"

"Next period," Keisha said. "Science. I thought you knew that."

"I don't know what I know," Bryce replied with a sigh. "I did my science homework, but I don't recognize what you're holding up."

"You don't?"

"Maybe it's my problem. I've been distracted lately. I can't stop thinking about gummy bears."

"Which is . . . completely normal," Keisha said.

"I know, right?" Bryce said. "Like, aren't

you always wondering what gummy bears would say if they could talk? It'd probably be 'Please don't eat me,' right? Could I possibly eat a gummy bear if it asked me not to? I'd like to say no, but I'm not sure I can do that. They're just so delicious."

While the morality of eating talking gummy bears was an utterly fascinating thing to ponder, Keisha kept her focus on homework.

"You said you did your homework, but you didn't recognize this worksheet?" she asked Bryce as she showed it to him again. "How can that be?"

Bryce dug into his backpack and pulled out his folded worksheet, which he slapped down on the table. As he unfolded it, Keisha noticed that it didn't match hers.

"Oh, I see the problem here," Bryce said. "You did the homework for *next* week. Mrs. Shen handed them both out on the same day, but you were supposed to do the other one first."

Keisha froze.

She stared straight ahead.

This couldn't be right.

"Are you okay?" Bryce asked.

She wasn't.

And she would get worse.

She reached into her backpack. She removed her homework folder, which was impressive . . . for a homework folder. It had numerous pockets for particular days and weeks. As she slowly opened it, Bryce spotted something.

"There's the right one," he said, pointing. "Looks like you put today's homework in the pocket for next week. I guess you got confused."

That's when Keisha stood up.

And that's when Keisha screamed.

At the top of her lungs.

Chapter Fifteen

THE ROAD TO CONSEQUENCE TOWN

Keisha's scream echoed through the art room, and everyone turned to look at her.

"Dagnammit!" Mr. Rao, the art teacher said. *Dagnammit* was a word he liked to use so he didn't have to swear in front of the whole class. Swearing in front of a class is never a good idea.

"Aaaaaaaah!" Keisha screamed again.

"Miss James, may I remind you that
we use our inside voices in this class?" Mr.
Rao said.

"AAAAAAAAAAAAAAAAH!"

Mr. Rao rushed over to her, his finger
wagging.

"Miss James! Miss James! I am
warning you. If you scream one more
time, you'll be—"

"AAAAAAAAAAA AAAAAAAAAAAAAAA AAAAAAH!"

It felt good to scream. In fact, it felt fantastic. But the consequences for screaming weren't going to feel so good.

Especially since while she was screaming, the clock fell out of Keisha's hand and . . .

Don't worry. It didn't break.

But also worry. Because it landed in a jar of red paint.

Chapter Sixteen

THE BUTTERFLY EFFECT

So the clock was covered in red paint because Keisha dropped it.

She dropped it because she was screaming.

She was screaming because she had traveled back in time over and over

again, struggling to find a handful
of free minutes in which to do her
homework, and then, what do you
know, she did the wrong homework.
Whoops.

Now Mr. Rao was going to send

her to Vice Principal
Meehan's office,
because he
didn't care about
red paint. Or
homework. Or time
travel. He cared only
about screaming.

There had been a reminder and
a warning. Now it was time for the

consequence. In other words, things were not going well for Keisha. But what, ultimately, was to blame for all this?

Simple. A butterfly.

This is not a joke. It all could be blamed on a butterfly. And it proves what is commonly called "the butterfly effect."

The butterfly effect is basically the following idea: A butterfly flapping its wings in China can cause a hurricane in Florida.

Seriously.

But perhaps it's best to clarify a few things:

1. No one is saying that a particular butterfly (or any butterfly, for that matter) has caused a hurricane. So please don't go yelling at random butterflies. Life is tough enough for them already.

Think about it.

They begin their lives waddling around as caterpillars, and then they suddenly have the urge to build this tiny little shell around themselves called a chrysalis. Which is weird, right? Then, when they build the chrysalis, they have to stay locked

inside it for days. Or even weeks! Without friends, family, or even a Wi-Fi signal. And sure, when they finally break out of the

chrysalis, they emerge as beautiful butterflies. But then they have to fly everywhere. Flying is tiring.

Monarch butterflies will confirm that fact. A lot of them fly from

Canada all the way to Mexico. Which is thousands of miles! And what do you think they do when they get there? Laze around on the beach, sipping lemonade?

Well, yes, sort of, but after a few months of vacation, they have to turn right back around and fly thousands of miles home. And when they get home, do they hug their families, have a pizza party, and get on with their lives?

Well, no, not even sort of.

They die.

So cut butterflies some slack.

2. Also, we're not saying that a butterfly can flap its wings so hard that a hurricane is created by nothing but the flapping. Because that would be one strong and terrifying butterfly.

If you're good at physics and biology and imagining gigantic monstrous butterflies, then maybe you can figure out how big a butterfly would have to be to cause a hurricane with wing flaps.

As big as a football stadium? That's

still probably too small, right?

As big as Camden, New Jersey? (If you don't know how big Camden, New Jersey, is, then just imagine it being as big as Pawtucket, Rhode Island. And everyone can imagine a Pawtucket-size butterfly, right?)

Or would it have to be even bigger? As big as Tuvalu? As big as San Marino? As big as Liechtenstein? Can you imagine? A butterfly as big as Liechtenstein? Every kid has nightmares about butterflies as big as Liechtenstein!

It ultimately doesn't matter, because there are no Liechtensteinian nightmare butterflies flapping around the globe and affecting our weather patterns.

Thank heavens.

3. But . . . and this is a big *but* . . . the idea that a butterfly can cause a hurricane cannot be ruled out. Because

the idea is that one small action can lead to bigger actions, which can lead to even bigger actions, which can lead to even bigger actions, and on and on and on, in a chain reaction, until something that seems meaningless ends up resulting in something that is truly monumental.

Of course, it's purely theoretical that a butterfly flapping its wings could set off a chain of events that would eventually cause a hurricane. But in Keisha's case, it *was* actually proven that a butterfly was to blame.

Seriously.

Chapter Seventeen
KEISHA'S BUTTERFLY

To understand a butterfly's role in Keisha's fate, we have to go back in time.

Not far. Only one day.

It was after school and Keisha was in her room, sitting at her desk, doing her homework. Her homework folder was open in front of her. She had finished her math and social studies homework. The only homework left was science. When all of a sudden—

Thwap. Thwap. Thwap.

There was a butterfly.

An orange-and-black butterfly was bumping into her window, trying to find its way outside. So Keisha stood up, and as she walked to the window, her elbow bumped against her desk fan. The bump turned the fan, which caused it to blow all the papers out of her homework folder.

Scrambling around her room, Keisha gathered up the papers and jammed them back in the folder. In the process, she put this week's homework in the following week's slot. And vice versa.

That was mistake number one.

Thwap. Thwap. Thwap.

The butterfly was still trying to escape. So when all the homework was gathered up and the fan was back in its original position, Keisha returned to the window. She opened it, the butterfly flew out, and that's when she saw—

Oh. My. Goodness.

A triple rainbow!

No one in their right mind would pass up the opportunity to photograph a single rainbow. So a person would have to be dead to pass up the opportunity to photograph a rare and wondrous triple rainbow.

Obviously, Keisha was bursting with life. She flew downstairs, hollering, "Gimme a phone! Triple rainbow! Triple rainbow!"

This was mistake number two.

Because as she flew downstairs,

grabbed her dad's phone, and went outside, Keisha's little brother, Kevin, slipped into her room.

Yes, Kevin was passing up the opportunity to photograph a triple rainbow. And no, he wasn't dead. So let's update that previous statement.

You'd have to be dead—*or* a sneaky little brother who really liked candy—to pass up the opportunity to photograph a triple rainbow. Because that's what was going on here. Kevin was trying to steal candy from his sister.

Kevin opened her desk drawers and moved all her papers in search of her stash of miniature bags of Skittles. He made quite a mess, tossing things here and there. Little did he know, the Skittles

were hidden away in her backpack.

When he heard the back door close and his sister entering the house, he panicked. He started stuffing objects back into drawers and stacking papers on her desk as neatly as he could. As for Keisha's homework folder, he dropped it into a slot above her desk that was labeled FINISHED.

When he heard Keisha bounding up the stairs, he slipped out as sneakily as he had slipped in. That's when she spotted him in the hall.

"You're missing the triple rainbow," she said.

"No, I'm missing the delicious rainbow of Skittles in my mouth, that's what I'm missing," Kevin grumbled under his breath.

"Excuse me?" Keisha said. "I didn't hear that."

Kevin flashed her a thumbs-up and replied, "Nothing, big sister. I was only talking about how lovely and brilliant you are."

If sarcasm was an art, then Kevin was one of Hopewell Elementary's finest artists. Keisha knew this well, and she knew not to encourage him. So she rolled her eyes and pushed past him and returned to her room.

What was I doing? she thought as she headed to her desk. *Homework, right?*

But when she saw that her homework folder was in the slot labeled FINISHED, she assumed she was finished. Because why else would it be there?

This was mistake number three.

"Dinner!" her father called from downstairs.

It was taco night, which was the best dinner night of the week. So Keisha flew back downstairs and didn't think about her science homework until Bryce mentioned it the next day.

As you can see, Keisha made three mistakes that led her to this point, but really it was a butterfly to blame.

Well, also a triple rainbow.

And a sneaky little brother who liked Skittles.

Chapter Eighteen
CONSEQUENCE TOWN

"AAAAAAAAAAAAAH!"

Remember, before we got distracted by all that butterfly stuff, Keisha was screaming. The reason she was screaming was because she didn't have her clock, and so she couldn't go back in time. Because also remember, the clock was in a jar of red paint.

"Good gravy, Miss James," Mr. Rao said. "This is ridiculous. You are disrupting the class. Please take a breath."

She did. She took three long, deep breaths. Then she looked around. Everyone was staring at her. She needed to explain herself.

"Okay, so get this, Mr. Rao," she said. "I forgot to do my science homework, and I was trying to do my science homework between classes. That meant running, jumping, hiding, distracting, Skittle-bombing, and being more or less amazing and superhuman. But it turns out I did the wrong science homework, and now I can't go back and do the right science homework because my clock is all blobbed up with red paint. Plus, I'm exhausted on account of the five extra hours in the day."

Everyone was silent and still. For a very, very long time.

"Okay," Mr. Rao finally said. "I was going to send you to Vice Principal Meehan's office, but instead, I think I'll send you to Nurse Bloom. It seems like you might . . . need that."

Mr. Rao was being very careful with his words. Keisha did not appear entirely healthy.

"Thank you," Keisha said, and then she grabbed the jar of red paint.

"And what do you have in your hand?" Mr. Rao asked, even though he could clearly see she was about to exit his classroom holding a jar of red paint.

"My clock," Keisha said. "Obviously, I wouldn't leave my clock behind."

"Obviously," Mr. Rao said. "And you obviously wouldn't want to get your *clock* all over anything. So please be careful with it."

"*Obviously*," Keisha said, and she headed for the door.

Chapter Nineteen
THE DUNGEON

Instead of going to Nurse Bloom's office, Keisha headed straight downstairs to the Dungeon.

Don't worry. Hopewell Elementary didn't have a medieval torture chamber in its basement. What it did have was a bathroom so dark, so dank, so unpleasant that kids called it the Dungeon.

Kids didn't use the Dungeon as an actual bathroom. Ugh. Gross. No, they used it as a place for mischief, and secret meetings about Locker 37, and washing red paint off tiny time-travel machines.

As Keisha approached the Dungeon, Carson was walking out. His shirt was soaking wet.

"What's going on?" she asked.

"I had a stain that I've been trying to get rid of all day," he said.

"Right," she said. "I knew that."

"You noticed?" he said with a gulp.

"You told me when I saw you at Locker 37."

"I remember seeing you there, but I don't remember saying that. You ran right past me."

"It was during a different timeline," Keisha explained. "Don't worry about it."

"Oh, I see," Carson said, trying, and failing, to understand. "So, did you find something in Locker 37 before I got there? Because when I opened it, it was empty."

Keisha considered what she might tell him. She wasn't sure the clock was going to work again, so she didn't want to tell him that she had messed up the one thing Locker 37 was giving out that day. But she also didn't want to lie.

"Sorry," she said. "I don't have much time left to talk."

Then she barreled into the Dungeon.

That's where she found Riley. Riley was rubbing her stomach and pacing beneath the Dungeon's flickering lights.

"I'm so hungry," she groaned.

"I haven't eaten anything all day. Cheesy breadsticks are the devil's food. I need fish sticks! I checked Locker 37, and it's empty. Fiiiiiish stiiiiiicks!"

"I wish I could help you," Keisha said. "But the only extra food I had were some bags of Skittles, and I already threw them all over the hallway."

"That was you?" Riley asked. "You know I fully support weird things. But that was a ridiculously weird thing to do."

Keisha shrugged. "You basically encouraged me to do it."

"I did?"

"Never mind," Keisha said. "Quick question: Are you going to be here for very long? Because I need to do something."

"Don't worry, I'll stay out of your way."

"Something *private*," Keisha said.

"Well, I can't exactly leave," Riley said. "Someone is bringing me fish sticks."

"Who would bring you fish sticks?"

"Me," a voice said.

The door creaked open. And there, standing at the entrance to the Dungeon, was Hunter Barnes.

He was holding a paper bag.

The bag was wet.

Chapter Twenty
FISH STICKS

"**S**o let me get this straight," Keisha said. "You are relying on Hunter Barnes to provide you with fish sticks?"

"His mom works in the cafetorium," Riley answered. "If there are fish sticks to be had, she's the person who can hook a girl up."

"And cook them, too?" Keisha asked.

"My mom will do anything for me," Hunter said with a grin. "Because she knows what a wonderful boy I am."

Riley rolled her eyes and added, "So wonderful that he's making me do his science homework for him in exchange for those fish sticks."

"What?!" Keisha yelled. "You're not allowed to do that! That's cheating!"

"Whoa, whoa, whoa, quiet down," Hunter said with his hands up. "Even if they're banging on bongo drums, I bet they can hear you yapping all the way up in the music room."

"Speaking of which," Keisha said, "shouldn't you two be in class right now?"

"Shouldn't you?" Hunter countered.

"We all should," Riley told them. "And I plan to as soon as I have my fish sticks."

"Then give it to me," Hunter said with a hand out.

Riley nodded and reached into her backpack. As she pulled out a completed science worksheet, Keisha was overcome by a dark feeling. What if she grabbed the worksheet and ran? She wouldn't need the clock anymore. She would have her finished homework, and who would really suffer?

So what if Riley didn't get her fish sticks? And so what if Hunter didn't have his homework? Did either of them deserve them? Had either of them struggled all day to get where they were?

No. Of course they hadn't. And yet, she couldn't take it.

Keisha knew that she should be the only person to blame for her failures. And the only person to credit for her successes. So she put her hands in her pockets and watched anxiously as Riley passed the worksheet to Hunter.

"Thank you very much," Hunter said as he snatched it and then tossed the paper bag on the counter by the sink. "Here are your fish . . . sticks."

Riley shot across the room as fast as she could, but by the time she had reached the bag, Hunter was gone. Which would come as no surprise.

"Holy potato gnocchi!" Riley yelled as she opened the bag.

She tipped it upside down.

A bunch of sticks fell out. Not fish

sticks, though. Regular sticks. Like from a
tree.

But that wasn't the only thing.

Two goldfish fell into the sink. And they were alive! They flopped around on the curved porcelain.

"Oh no!" Keisha yelled. "Is that . . . is that . . . Finn and Gill?"

And as she reached to grab them, they slipped down the drain.

Chapter Twenty-One

A PLUMBING DILEMMA

It was indeed Finn and Gill. Keisha noticed the distinctive white marks on their tails right before they disappeared down the drain. Unfortunately, there was only one sink in the Dungeon. So Keisha had to make a decision.

Did she turn on the tap so that she could wash the paint off the clock?

Turning the tap on would surely flush

the fish through the pipes, and they'd end
up somewhere that was very disgusting
and very dangerous. They probably
wouldn't survive the journey. But if she

got the clock working again, she could also save them. She could go back in time to the beginning of the day and protect Finn and Gill.

Keisha got down on her hands and knees to look at the pipes under the sink.

"You haven't become a plumber in the last few weeks, have you?" she asked Riley.

"What? No. Why would I become a plumber?" Riley said.

"Kids have hobbies," Keisha said. "I'm president and founding member of the Junior Janitor Club."

"Yes, I know, and you seem to be very proud of the fact," Riley remarked. "Though I can't figure out why."

"Because the world can always be

cleaner, Riley," Keisha said. "It can always be cleaner. But that's beside the point. The point is, you're not a plumber and I'm not a plumber and neither of us has a pipe wrench on us and I don't how long those poor fish were in that bag, and I don't know how long they can survive in that pipe, and so right now we're wasting time that we could be using washing *this*."

She held up the blob of red that was the clock.

Riley put her hands up and backed away.

"Clearly you're thinking on a whole other level," Riley said. "So I'll just let you wash your red blobby thingy, or whatever, while I go tell the janitor about our goldfish emergency."

"His name is Reggie Blue," Keisha said as she held the clock under the tap.

"What? Who?"

"The janitor. Tell Reggie it's a favor for me. Now go! And Godspeed."

Godspeed means good luck, but Riley figured it meant to go, well, as fast as God. And while she wasn't quite that fast, she was out of the Dungeon by the time Keisha had turned the tap on.

"Come on, come on, come on," Keisha said as she washed the clock.

Most of the red paint had dried, but she managed to peel some clumps off the top until she found the knob.

She washed and washed and washed some more until the knob was somewhat clean.

Then she leaned forward and spoke into the sink.

"Hang in there, Gill and Finn, wherever you are."

She pulled out the knob, but it didn't click.

She wound it backward, but it was difficult to move. The paint must have found its way inside and among the gears.

When she couldn't wind it back anymore, she crossed her fingers and pressed the knob in.

Chapter Twenty-Two
WHEN AM I?

*P*ffffffff...

Keisha was running. Down a hall, it appeared. She looked at her clock to see what time it was. But she couldn't read it. Because—you know—paint!

The sun was high in the sky, shining through windows at the end of the hall. She could at least guess that this wasn't the beginning of the day. So when was she?

She stopped and asked Nina Camacho. "What time is it?"

"Seriously," Nina said. "You don't know? You always have your day planned out to the second."

"The only plan I have right now is to save Finn and Gill, so tell me what time it is. Is it ten? Eleven?"

Nina gasped. "You don't even know the hour?"

It felt miserable to be confused, but Keisha wasn't going to take that out on Nina, even if Nina wasn't exactly being sympathetic. Keisha simply gritted her teeth and shook her head.

"We just had lunch," Nina said with a little giggle. "Did your mom pack a forgetting potion with your PBJ?"

If lunch had just ended, it meant Keisha was on her way to math. Math was in Mrs. Shen's room. This was good. Very good. She could check on Finn and Gill.

"Thank you for being so kind and understanding, Nina," Keisha said, channeling some of the sarcasm her little brother was known for. "Sorry, but I can't stay to chat. Got goldfish to save."

Then Keisha was off, running faster than she'd run all day.

When she reached Mrs. Shen's room, Finn and Gill were still swimming in their bowl.

"Oh, that's a relief," she said.

"You're relieved that you're the first one to arrive?" Mrs. Shen asked. "But you're always first to class."

Keisha hurried over to the bowl and kissed the glass. "I don't care about being first as long as these two are safe."

"Well, I don't think they're about to go anywhere. They're a bit limited in that regard."

"To be sure about that," Keisha said, "is there a way to lock them into this bowl? You know, so no one can steal them?"

"Why would anyone steal Finn and Gill?"

"To put them in a paper bag with a pile of sticks in an attempt to obtain illicit science homework," Keisha said as she wrapped her arms around the bowl.

"I . . . see," Mrs. Shen said. "Are you feeling okay, Keisha?"

"Honestly?"

"Honestly."

"I'm tired, Mrs. Shen. But I have a responsibility. And right now my responsibility is to make sure these fish are safe."

"Fair enough," Mrs. Shen said. "But please still pay attention in class, will you?"

"I said I'm tired, Mrs. Shen. Not dead."

Chapter Twenty-Three
HUNTER'S SECRET

The tired, but not dead, Keisha James stood guard over the fish. And as soon as Hunter entered Mrs. Shen's classroom, she pointed at him.

"Get within five feet of these fish, Hunter, and I swear you will regret it," she said.

Hunter, who seemed to forget who he was dealing with for a moment, smirked and asked, "How am I gonna regret it?"

Keisha had had her devastating comeback ready since the bus that morning. And the reason that comeback was so devastating was because Keisha knew something about Hunter that no one else in fourth grade knew.

Granted, this was not something Keisha was supposed to know. But as president of the Junior Janitor Club, she emptied a lot of overflowing trash cans. And at the end of the first day of fourth grade, Keisha was taking a small trash can out to the dumpster when she found that the dumpster was missing.

Rather than leave the trash in the school, Keisha took the contents of the can home with her, where she sorted through it to remove anything recyclable.

This is how she found a letter.

In that letter, she found some difficult news.

She tried not to read the entire thing, because she didn't want to invade someone else's privacy, but she saw enough to know that it concerned Hunter. Actually, she saw enough to know it was about how he was struggling so much in school that he was almost held back in third grade. The letter said that if he had another difficult year, he would definitely be held back in fourth grade.

So when Hunter asked, "How am I gonna regret it?" Keisha responded in a snarky tone.

"Let me ask you a question," she said.

"If you could go back and do third grade all over again, would you? What about fourth grade?"

Blood rushed to Hunter's cheeks. The question clearly made him nervous, and he stuttered his response. "Like ... like ... go back ... if I had a ... had a time machine?" he asked.

"Sure," Keisha said with a smile. "A time machine is the only way you would have to repeat fourth grade, correct?"

Hunter didn't answer right away. He simply

stepped away from the fishbowl. Then he asked, "Am I five feet from it now?"

"That'll do," Keisha said.

As Hunter sat down at a desk far away from her, Keisha reached into her pocket and felt the clock.

Was that too cruel? she wondered.

Should I go back and try to stop Hunter in a kinder way?

Or did Locker 37 give me the power of time travel so I could be mean to him?

It was hard to say, because Locker 37 never explained its solutions.

Every day, it provided kids with an object that solved their problems. Most of the solutions were self-explanatory. Such as the times it gave out:

- A happily haunted hairbrush that fixed bad hairdos. Bowl cuts, botched dye jobs, even uneven bangs. It was like a salon on a stick!

- A bewilderingly bewitched bagel that a hungry kid could eat all day and there would always be more bagelly goodness to eat. Cream cheese and lox were optional, of course, because infinite lox is a bit too much lox.

- Some eerily enchanted earmuffs that kept the wearer warm no matter how cold it was and no matter how few clothes they had on. Socks and undies all you got? No problem with these cozy wonders, though a pair of pants and shirt are still suggested if you're planning on going to class.

Those objects solved problems immediately, and kids went on their merry ways.

But some problems required more complicated solutions. Keisha's problem, for instance, required time travel. Locker 37 wasn't about to explain why exactly. It was Keisha's job to figure that part out.

One thing was for sure, though. This

was a big deal for Locker 37.

In its many years of service, it had given out a time-travel device only once before. And the results were . . . interesting.

Chapter Twenty-Four

THE CURIOUS CASE OF MORTIMER SCHNELL

More than fifty years before Keisha went to Hopewell Elementary, there was a boy named Mortimer Schnell who walked its halls.

This Mortimer Schnell kid was a real scoundrel.

MORTIMER

TOTAL KNOW-IT-ALL

LARRY

SCHOOL BULLY

What that means is that he was a bit of a mischief-maker and a bit of a villain. A lot like Hunter Barnes, come to think of it. But Mortimer Schnell was smarter than Hunter.

One autumn morning of his fourth-grade year, Mortimer brought his pet snake, Larry, to school for show-and-tell. Mortimer thought there'd be no harm in it, but I think you can see where this is going.

Larry escaped. Obviously.

And then Larry proceeded to eat not one, not two, but three of the school's hamsters.

This was a bad thing. Obviously.

Even though Mortimer Schnell was a scoundrel, he had a conscience. He truly loved animals. So he ran to Locker 37 to get a solution.

Locker 37 gave him a spinning top.

The top was a time-travel device, and whenever Mortimer spun it, it would send him back in time to a few moments before Larry escaped. So while it wasn't as precise as Keisha's clock, it did the trick.

Etched around the edge of the top was a message: *Three Spins Only*

On his first spin, Mortimer saved the hamsters and continued on with his day. Simple enough. But during last period, Mortimer's teacher gave the class a surprise test. It was called the TWIT, which stood for The Worldwide Intelligence Test.

Mortimer was smart, but the TWIT

was the hardest test he had ever taken. He didn't get a single question right on the whole thing!

It ultimately didn't matter. His teacher told the class that the TWIT wasn't a test for grades. It was merely designed to locate the smartest kids in the country. But that only made things worse. Because Mortimer was competitive. And since he was also a scoundrel, he devised a plan. He spun the top again.

On this go-around, he saved the hamsters again. Obviously. But when his teacher gave the class the TWIT, Mortimer didn't spend his time answering the questions. He spent his time memorizing them.

Then he gave the top its final spin.

He saved the hamsters again. Of course. But most of his day was spent trying to figure out the answers to the impossible questions he had memorized.

This was before the Internet was invented, so he had to do it the old-fashioned way.

By going to the library?

No. By asking someone smarter.

He ran out to a pay phone at the front of the school and called his brother, Phineas, who was in college at MIT (which is one of the best colleges in the country, in case you didn't know). Mortimer told Phineas that he'd give him his allowance for two months if he could figure out the answers to the questions.

Phineas had a lot of smart friends and professors to help out, and Mortimer's allowance was substantial, so Phineas accepted his brother's challenge.

Flash forward to the end of the day and about twenty minutes before the test. Mortimer ran back outside to the pay phone. He called Phineas again.

"It wasn't easy, but I got all the answers," Phineas told him. "You're gonna ace this thing, little brother."

And Mortimer did. He aced that TWIT. In fact, he got a perfect score!

The spinning top disappeared, never to be used again. And that was all right by Mortimer, because everything seemed to go perfectly.

That is, until a week later . . . when the head of NASA showed up at Hopewell Elementary.

"You are the only person who has ever gotten a perfect score on the TWIT," the head of NASA said to Mortimer, "so you must be a genius of the highest order."

"Well," Mortimer replied, "I'm not

going to brag, but yeah, I'm pretty much the smartest person in the universe."

"That remains to be seen," the big powerful NASA guy said, "but we shall see it soon enough. Young Master Schnell, we are taking you out of school and putting you in a job. Your parents have given us their blessings. Arrangements have been made. We leave this very instant."

Then the NASA dude led Mortimer to a white van in front of the school and drove him away.

No one at Hopewell Elementary saw or heard from Mortimer Schnell again.

Chapter Twenty-Five

PERHAPS, MAYBE, POSSIBLY

So what was the purpose of the spinning top?

To save the hamsters? Sure, it could be. But was it also trying to make sure Mortimer Schnell left school? And if so, why?

Maybe it was punishing him for

being dishonest. Did the people at NASA soon discover how unexceptional he really was? Did it lead to such a colossal embarrassment for everybody that Mortimer decided never to return to Hopewell Elementary?

Or maybe NASA really needed him. Coincidentally or not, this all happened shortly before NASA put the first human on the moon. So was it possible that the lying, cheating Mortimer Schnell had a hand in that singular achievement?

It was possible. But impossible to know for sure.

Locker 37 was an enigma. That basically meant it wasn't giving up any of its secrets. However, one thing was clear. It didn't hand out time-travel devices all willy-nilly after that. It was more than fifty years later that it gave Keisha her clock. So what made Keisha so special?

In some ways, Keisha was similar to Mortimer. She was relentless and clever like he was. In other ways, she was the opposite. She was honorable. She did not cheat.

Locker 37 thought she was deserving of a time-travel device, but there were other ways it could have helped her finish her homework. How about a time-stopping device, for instance? Over the years, it had given out plenty of those. If Locker 37 had given Keisha a time-stopping clock instead, she could have frozen time for thirty minutes or so, finished her homework, and gotten on with her day.

So perhaps, maybe, possibly it was only partly about the homework?

Chapter Twenty-Six

THE COMMON GOOD

Once math was over and Hunter had left the room, Keisha approached Mrs. Shen.

"I'd like to take Finn and Gill with me if that's okay," she told her.

"That's highly unusual," Mrs. Shen said.

"But is it okay?" Keisha asked.

"I suppose, but I'm not sure your other teachers will agree. They might see Finn and Gill as a distraction."

"True," Keisha said. "But there's Hunter Barnes to think about. He can't know their whereabouts, can he?"

A puzzled look swept over Mrs. Shen's face, but Keisha didn't worry about that because she suddenly realized the solution.

"You know what?" she said. "I think I got this."

Problem was, Keisha would need all five minutes before both recess and art to do what had to be done. Which meant she had to run. Again.

And the other problem was, she had the fishbowl. Try running with a fishbowl without spilling any water. Spoiler alert: Your floors will be wet.

But there
would be no wet
floors in Hopewell
Elementary that day.
Because remember,
Keisha had a plan.

She started
pulling the rubber
bands from her hair, and her homework
folder from her backpack. She placed
the folder over the top of the fishbowl
and wrapped the rubber bands around
it, creating a secure roof.

"What are you doing?" Mrs. Shen
asked.

"Trust me."

"I do trust you, Keisha. As much as I
trust anyone. But answer me this one

question. If I trust you this time, will I regret it?"

"You will not, Mrs. Shen. Believe me. This is for the common good."

Then she patted Mrs. Shen on the shoulder, grabbed the covered fishbowl, and sprinted out of the room.

She went directly to the janitor closet that was down the hall from Locker 37, where she reached into her backpack and pulled out her set of janitor keys. She slipped a key into the doorknob, unlocked the door, and opened it. She set the fishbowl down for a moment as she moved some laundry detergent across a shelf in the back of the closet. Then she placed the fishbowl on the shelf and slid the laundry detergent in front of it, effectively hiding the fish.

"You'll be safe in here," she told Finn and Gill.

Then she shut the door and locked it. And she ran as fast as she could to recess.

But there's something strange going on here, right? Why on earth would a fourth-grader have a set of janitor keys?

Such questions show that you haven't been reading carefully enough. Did you miss that Keisha was a member of the Junior Janitor Club? Did you miss that she'd already used the janitor keys?

But Junior Janitor Club isn't really a thing, is it? Elementary schools don't have janitor clubs, do they?

Such questions show that even if you

haven't been reading carefully enough,
at least you have been thinking clearly
enough.

No, Junior Janitor Club is not really a
thing. Especially in elementary schools.
That is, except at Hopewell Elementary.
Because that's where Keisha went. And
that's where Keisha made the whole
thing up.

Keisha hated messes. And the school janitor, who was a hardworking man named Reggie Blue, had a lot of ground to cover in Hopewell Elementary. Not every spilled drink or piece of litter could be dealt with immediately. So Keisha and Reggie forged a deal. Keisha could have access to the janitor closets and all their cleaning supplies, as long as she agreed to clean up any messes she saw.

It was a good deal for Reggie.

It was a good deal for Keisha, too. At least in her mind. The school was tidier, plus she had an extra extracurricular activity to brag about and put on her application for college.

Granted, Keisha was the founder, president, vice president, secretary, treasurer, and sole member of the Junior Janitor Club. But her membership privileges were finally paying off. She now had the perfect place to hide the fish. However, there were only two class periods left and not enough time to finish her homework.

She had recess, though. Could she sacrifice recess for the sake of homework?

Chapter Twenty-Seven
RECESS

Keisha would have to sacrifice recess. It felt like the only choice that remained. It was hard to tell if the clock would work again, and if it did, how far back it would take her. Did she have the energy to do it all again?

No, she didn't. Sorry, recess.

It was a lovely day outside. Kids were swarming the playground structures and flying high on the swings. A game of capture the flag had started near the sandbox. And there were at least five different people pretending to be superheroes and running around with arms outstretched.

So yes, it was lovely. But it was also loud. Thankfully, at the edge of the playground, there was a wonderfully gnarled willow tree. It provided shade, privacy, and best of all, quiet. So that's where Keisha went. She'd risk being caught by the monitors. It was all she could do.

She eased her body down and placed her back against the trunk. It felt glorious to relax. Clouds were puffy in the sky, and they seemed to swirl and dance, and Keisha watched them for a few moments, hoping it would clear her head.

It did. Completely.

It cleared her head for at least thirty minutes. Until . . .

"Keisha."

"Keisha."

"Keisha!"

Voices were all around her. It was super dark. But that wasn't surprising. Her eyes were closed.

When she opened them, three figures came into focus: Carson, Riley, and Bryce.

"She's awake!" Carson announced.

"Oh good," Riley said. "I thought she might be dead. That would've been awkward."

"I never thought you could nap at

recess," Bryce said. "Is napping allowed?"

"I wasn't napping," Keisha said. "I was resting my eyes."

"You were resting your eyes for half an hour at least," Riley said. "Every time I looked over here, you were resting your eyes. And now recess is over."

That couldn't be possible. Keisha felt like she'd sat down only seconds before. "Did I travel forward in time?" she asked.

"Napping is pretty much like time travel," Bryce said. "Close your eyes and *zzzzzzzap*, it could be ten minutes later. It could be ten hours."

"You've napped ten hours?" Carson asked.

"Only at night," Bryce said.

"That's called sleeping," Keisha said as she stood and dusted herself off. "Did I really miss all of recess?"

"Sure did," Riley said. "And we're all

going to miss art unless we make a run for it."

"We have to run . . . again?" Keisha said with a sigh.

"Yep," Riley said. "Last one there is Hunter's undies."

And they were off.

Chapter Twenty-Eight
ART CLASS AGAIN

Keisha was panting and sweating when she arrived at art class, but as she took her seat, she tried to remember something positive.

The fish were safe. That was good.

But that memory sparked another memory.

Her homework folder was still attached to the top of the fishbowl. Yikes.

There was no possible way to finish her homework now. That was bad.

So when Bryce sat down next to her, Keisha couldn't wave her homework in the air and brag like last time. She could only say, "This might be the one time in history that you beat me, Bryce."

"Beat you at what?" Bryce asked.

"I don't know. Life."

"I'm not so sure about that. Things are pretty confusing for me right now."

"Oh, right," Keisha said. "Gummy bears."

"Gummy bears," Bryce echoed with a sigh. "I've been checking all day, but not even Locker 37 can help me figure out if I should be eating gummy bears. I wish one would just tell me it was okay."

It was such a weird thing to be obsessed with. But then again, weren't a lot of obsessions weird? Keisha had spent the entire day obsessed with what? Finishing a science worksheet? It had seemed like the most important thing in the world to her earlier. But now?

Now she had to be satisfied with saving the fish. That was her big accomplishment. All the extra hours added to her day had taken their toll. She couldn't even stay awake. As horrible as it might have once seemed, she simply had to accept that she wouldn't get the homework done.

Meanwhile, at the front of the classroom, Carson was whispering to Mr. Rao. Mr. Rao was handing him a hall pass.

And Carson was holding his arm across his shirt, covering up the stain.

It was sad. It was only a stain. But again, everyone has obsessions that are hard to understand. Keisha wished she could help, but—

But what? Why couldn't she help? She still had a time machine in her pocket! Maybe it wouldn't work, but she at least had to give it a shot. Because her obsession was no more important than Carson's. And his obsession was easily fixed. The solution was in the janitor closet, right in front of the fish. Laundry detergent!

As exhausted as she was, she knew what she had to do.

"I might fall asleep on the job," Keisha

said out loud, to no one in particular. "And who knows if this red paint has done too much damage to my clock. But, dagnammit, it's time to make today better than the today before, okay?"

Her classmates confronted her with blank stares.

"Don't worry about it, everybody," she said as she pulled out the knob on the clock. "Especially you, Carson."

Carson stopped at the door, his arm over his chest. "Huh?" he said.

"I got you, buddy," Keisha said, and she twisted the knob as hard as she could, hoping to break through whatever globs of paint were gunking up the gears inside. "I got you."

The clock made squealing sounds.

And snapping sounds.

And what almost sounded like groaning.

Keisha managed to turn the knob a lot more than she had the time before.

But when she pushed the knob in . . .

Chapter Twenty-Nine

WHERE'S THE BEEF?

The clock broke.

It fell apart. Every last bit of it. Springs and gears and hands and the glass burst into a mess on Keisha's palm and then tumbled to the floor.

But it wasn't the floor in the art room. It was the floor in the hallway outside of Locker 37.

Keisha turned to see Carson walking toward her.

"What are you doing here?" she asked.

"I was sorta hoping to use Locker 37," Carson said. "But I guess you beat me to it."

It was the exact same conversation she had had multiple times before. She had successfully traveled back to the beginning of the day. Which meant the clock might have been broken, but it had still worked.

It had worked! One final time. And it was time to make that time count.

"I'm gonna need your shirt," she told Carson, and she paced toward him.

"What?"

"No time to waste. Come with me."

Keisha led Carson through the halls until they reached the janitor closet. She pulled out her janitor keys.

"What are you doing?" he asked.

"Helping you."

"This looks like trouble. I don't think we're supposed to be in here. I don't think you're supposed to be doing this."

As she opened the door and grabbed laundry detergent off the shelf, she said, "I'm the president of the Junior Janitor Club, for crying out loud. What I'm supposed to do is make a difference in this school. And so that's exactly what I'm doing. Now follow me."

Next, she led him to an unmarked door. Again, the janitor keys did the trick and unlocked it.

"Take off your shirt," she said as she pushed the door open.

"What? No. Where are we?"

Keisha sighed, pulled Carson through the door, and turned on a light. "Voilà," she said.

They were in a laundry room. There were at least three industrial-size washers and six massive dryers.

"You will give me your shirt," she went on. "I will wash it and dry it and have it back to you by lunch."

"But I don't have anything else to wear," Carson said.

Keisha hurried to the back of the room and pulled a partly torn cardboard box off a rickety shelf. The box was piled with clothes.

"This is what's known as the Mountain of Forgotten Clothes. They're all unclaimed items from the Lost and Found. A lot of it is pretty cool, actually. Some of it is decades old. Vintage."

Carson dipped his hand in and pulled out a T-shirt. It said *Where's the Beef?* on the front.

"What does that mean?" he asked.

"I don't know," Keisha said. "Someone lost their beef, I guess."

"Better than nothing."

Two minutes later, Keisha and Carson stepped back into the hall. The washer

was washing Carson's stain away, and he was wearing the *Where's the Beef?* T-shirt.

The janitor, Reggie Blue, stood outside with his arms crossed. "What's doin', K?" he asked Keisha.

"Nothin', Reg," she said. "Helping a fellow student. We gotta get back to class, but I started a load if you have any clothes that need cleaning."

"All good here, Madam Pres," Reggie said with a salute, and then he turned to Carson. "Cool shirt, Ace."

"You think so?" Carson asked.

"I know so."

Which made Carson smile. And that made Keisha happy.

Chapter Thirty

A TALKING GUMMY BEAR

When Keisha returned to music class, Bryce waved to her. She had expected that.

And Mr. Gregson was pointing to lyrics on the whiteboard, which was something she had also expected.

But as she ducked in front of the whiteboard, she looked up at it for the first time that day and saw one of the lyrics to the song "Time After Time."

If you fall, I will catch you, I'll be waiting.

Something struck her. Catching someone was the same as helping someone.

She had gone through this day so many times already that she knew exactly where to be waiting to "catch" people. She had done it for Carson, so why couldn't she do it for others?

Bryce, for instance. In this new timeline, he hadn't mentioned gummy bears to Keisha yet. So Keisha was going to use that to her advantage . . . and his!

"Hey, Bryce," she whispered as she joined him onstage. "I have something weird to tell you."

"I like weird," Bryce whispered back.

"So I was talking with a gummy bear this morning, and he asked me to tell you 'it's fine.'"

It's fine!

Bryce's eyes went wide. He took a deep breath. He took two deep breaths. His hands shook. "Are you serious?" he whispered.

"Totally," Keisha whispered. "I mean, I've talked to animal crackers before, but this was the first gummy bear.

And I wasn't sure what he meant by 'it's fine.' But maybe you do?"

"I do, I do. I really, really do," Bryce yelped.

He yelped it too loudly, however.

Because Mr. Gregson cleared his throat and said, "Miss James and Mr. Dodd, unless you are discussing the lyrics to the immortal classic 'Time After Time,' then I kindly ask you to shut . . . your . . . mouths. This is your reminder."

"I'm sorry, Mr. Gregson," Keisha replied. "Bryce is such a big fan of the Screamin' Beagles and he's beyond excited that we get to sing one of the songs your band performs so well."

This was the truth, but it was a creative truth.

And it made Mr. Gregson smile. Which he didn't often do.

"Thank you, Bryce, that's very kind," Mr. Gregson said. "But let's quiet down and focus on learning the lyrics, okay?"

"Sure thing," Bryce said with a nod. "And Keisha is right. The Screamin' Beagles are possibly the greatest band in history."

Bryce smiled again, which made Mr. Gregson smile again.

That made Keisha smile, too.

Chapter Thirty-One

SMILES ALL AROUND

It felt fantastic to make people smile. Keisha wanted that feeling again.

As she left music, she went through the details of every timeline she had experienced, remembering all the things she had seen in the hallway while she was running. Some things had changed from timeline to timeline, but some things remained consistent.

Like Hayley Baker tripping over
her untied shoelaces and falling in the
hall. That was going to happen in a few
seconds!

So Keisha ran over and jumped in
front of her.

"Oh, hey," Hayley said. "Didn't see you
there, Keisha."

Keisha reached into her backpack and
pulled out a bag of Skittles. She dropped it
on Hayley's untied shoe. "Those Skittles are
all yours if you tie your shoe," she said.

Hayley looked down, then at Keisha,
then down again, and then at Keisha
again.

"You're giving me candy to tie my own
shoe?"

"Yes," Keisha said. "But only if you

double knot it. I can't have you falling over in the hall."

Hayley smiled. Keisha did, too. Then Keisha patted her on the shoulder and kept walking.

The rest of the day proceeded in a similar fashion.

Keisha went to classes, and even though she was exhausted, she excelled, as usual.

But this time she didn't run between classes. And she didn't have time to work on homework. Because she was too busy helping people.

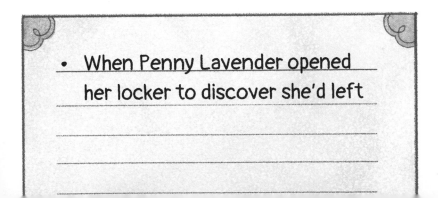

- When Penny Lavender opened her locker to discover she'd left her math book at home, Keisha was there waiting with an extra copy . . . and some Skittles.

- When Devon Garcia sneezed and snuffled in the back of social studies, Keisha had a pack of tissues ready for her . . . along with some Skittles.
- When Rajib Mohanty bent over to take a drink from the drinking fountain that dribbled water, Keisha grabbed his shoulder to stop him. "Don't put your mouth on that germ factory, my friend," she said. "Here, enjoy this instead." And she handed him a bottle of water . . . and some Skittles.

Smiles all around.

She also returned Carter's stain-free shirt, hot from the dryer. But he didn't put it on because his *Where's the Beef?* shirt was such a hit with the teachers for some reason.

It was turning out to be a fabulous day, but Keisha's greatest victory was still to come.

Lunch.

Chapter Thirty-Two
HEARTBREAKING TIME-TRAVEL ASSUMPTIONS

Want to hear something sad?
Many people think humans will never figure out how to travel backward in time.

"Oh my goodness, that is sad," you're probably saying.

You're probably also saying it's

wrong, right? Because isn't traveling back in time exactly what Keisha did?

The thing is, many people don't know about Keisha. And some of those many people have proposed the following theory:

If humans had learned how to travel back in time, then we would've met them by now.

How do they figure that?

Well, let's think of time as something you can explore, like you can explore the earth. Humans have been exploring the earth for thousands of years. And in the last hundred of those years, we've gotten quite good at it. Cars and airplanes and hoverboards are wonderful inventions, after all. If you've got the money and the desire, you can start your day in New Delhi, India, and end it in Fairbanks, Alaska.

Humans have been to the tops of the highest mountains, to the bottoms of the deepest oceans. Even the people who live in the heart of the jungle, or high up in the Arctic ice, know there are other people out there in the world.

So let's look at time in the same way. If we assume that humans will eventually invent a time-travel machine, then we can assume they're going to want to explore the entire past, right? Exactly like we've explored the entire earth?

The theory proposes that eventually time travelers would've explored the era we're in right now, and we'd at least know about the existence of travelers

from other times. Exactly like how people in Wonglepong, Australia, know there are people in Boogertown, North Carolina. A Wongleponger might've even met a Boogertonian, because so many corners of our earth have been explored by so many people.

However, since there isn't a time-traveler tourist center in every town on earth, we can make one of the following assumptions:

1. **The heartbreaking assumption:** Even if Locker 37 occasionally hands out very limited time-travel devices, the human race will go extinct before we figure out how to make our own

time-travel machines that will allow us to visit our ancestors.

2. **The less heartbreaking, but still heartbreaking, assumption:** Humans will eventually make our own time-travel machines, but we won't use them to travel to certain eras in human history (right now, for instance), because those eras are too *booooooooring.*

3. **The assumption that breaks . . . fewer hearts:** Humans will eventually make our own time-travel machines, and we will travel to every era in human history. But no one from the past will figure it out because, come on,

time travelers are smart enough not to reveal themselves.

If we assume assumption number three, then we have to wonder where these mysterious time travelers are hiding. Well, there's one obvious answer to that.

In elementary school cafetoriums.

Chapter Thirty-Three

THE CAFETORIUM CONUNDRUM

Why cafetoriums?

Simple. When you travel to another town or another country, where is a place you almost always go?

Wherever there's food, of course. Restaurants, markets, cafetoriums. There's the practical reason: You have to eat to survive. But there's also the educational reason: What better way is there to know about a culture than to watch people eat and interact (and put on the occasional Cyndi Lauper tribute concert)?

So that's why it's safe to assume that at least some of the people in elementary school cafetoriums are time travelers. And they are here to learn about children because children are the most interesting humans in the world. Frankly, to assume anything else would be utterly foolish.

And who might those time travelers be? Well, the people who serve the food. Because who else could it be?

Of course, Keisha had no reason to

suspect there were any time travelers in the cafetorium serving up cheesy breadsticks. But when she arrived at lunch, still smiling from all the happiness she had spread in Hopewell Elementary, she did have a reason to suspect there were still more smiles to spread.

Near the back of the cafetorium, next to a cart of dirty trays and plates, Hunter and Riley were deep in conversation. They were gesturing, squinting, scratching their chins. It was serious stuff. And Keisha knew exactly what it was about.

Fish sticks.

For a moment, Keisha felt anger trying to push the happiness from her body. Because she flashed back to the future, to the Dungeon, to Finn and Gill flopping around in the sink and slipping down the drain.

And she was tempted to run up to Hunter and grab him by the collar and say awful things. She was tempted to stand on a table and announce to the whole school that Hunter was in danger of being held back a grade. Quite frankly, she was tempted to punch him in the gut.

But try as it might, the anger couldn't overpower the happiness, and Keisha didn't give in to temptation. She had a better way to deal with things. She hurried to the lunch line instead.

Grabbing a carton of milk, she made her way to the register, where Hunter's mom was entering kids' account numbers.

"Hello, Mrs. Barnes," Keisha said. "How are you on this most interesting day?"

"I am very well, thank you, Keisha," Mrs. Barnes said.

"Let me get straight to the point," Keisha said. "I am buying this milk, but I am here for a bigger reason. And that reason is your son, Hunter."

Mrs. Barnes's face dropped. "Oh no. What now?"

"Don't worry, he hasn't done anything wrong today," Keisha said. "At least not yet. And to make sure he doesn't, I'm going to need some fish sticks."

"I'm sorry, what?"

"Fish sticks, Mrs. Barnes. It's a very

complicated situation, but lives are at stake, and I know that fish sticks are in short supply. But a single, or better yet a double, helping will make all the difference. You must have a hidden stash that you can cook up for me, right?"

Mrs. Barnes's eyes narrowed. "I'm not sure I understand. It's cheesy breadstick day. That's what we're serving."

Keisha had been hoping it wouldn't come to this, but she decided to pull out all the stops. "I tell you what," she said. "I ride the bus with Hunter. And I notice that sometimes he's a little, shall we say, *behind* in his homework. Here's what I propose. I will tutor him on the bus every morning for the next month. In exchange, you will get me some of those disgusting, revolting,

nauseating fish sticks. And please make sure they're cooked to, well, not perfection exactly, because they couldn't possibly be perfect. But cooked whatever way weirdos who eat fish sticks like them cooked."

Mrs. Barnes's eyes narrowed even more. "You're serious?"

"Yes," Keisha said. "Tired as well. So I'm willing to do what it takes. And that means making your son a better student."

There was no one else in the line behind Keisha, so it was safe for

Mrs. Barnes to leave her post. After taking some time to consider Keisha's proposal, that's exactly what she did.

"Wait here a minute," Mrs. Barnes said, and she walked back into the kitchen.

About fifty seconds later, she returned. And wouldn't you know it? She was carrying a tray of fish sticks, so hot that steam was rising from them.

"Wait," Keisha said. "How did you do that so fast?"

With a mischievous smile, Mrs. Barnes said, "Our convection oven is so fast that it might as well be a time machine."

Keisha laughed awkwardly. "If only time machines existed," she said.

"If only," Mrs. Barnes said with a wider smile as she passed the tray to Keisha.

Chapter Thirty-Four
DELIVERY

Was Hunter's mom a time traveler? Did she go back in time to put the fish sticks in the convection oven so that they'd be hot and ready for Keisha exactly when she needed them? Or was the convection oven really that fast?

It's impossible to say. Convection ovens are that mysterious. And lunch ladies and time travelers and time-traveling lunch ladies don't reveal their secrets. Not even to their sons.

To Hunter, she was simply a mom, and one he cared a great deal about.

So when Keisha approached Hunter and Riley with the tray of fish sticks, he said, "You weren't giving my mom a hard time over there, were you, Keisha?"

"No," Keisha said. "She was giving me these."

Drool dripped from Riley's mouth, and her hand started to move toward the tray. "How did you . . . ? Can I have . . . ? Would you give me . . . one?"

There was no reason to tempt Riley any more, so Keisha handed her the tray. "They're all yours." Then she reached into her bag and grabbed her last two packages of Skittles. "And so are these."

She handed one bag to Hunter and one to Riley.

"What's this for?" Hunter asked.

"You won't be cheating your way to finished science homework today," Keisha said as she patted him on the shoulder. "But you're not alone. Because neither will I."

"You didn't do the science homework?"

Keisha shrugged and said, "Nobody's perfect. But we'll make sure it doesn't happen again. For either of us. I'm going to help you, Hunter. Tutor you. On the bus. Every day for the next month. Whattaya say?"

Hunter was stunned into silence.

"I'll take that as a yes," Keisha told him.

Then she turned to Riley so she could

witness one more smiling face for the day.

But Riley wasn't smiling. She was too busy gobbling down the fish sticks faster than seemed humanly possible.

It was super gross. It was also better than a smile.

Chapter Thirty-Five
WHAT IS TIME?

When Keisha arrived at math class for the last time that day, she sat down next to Finn and Gill. Their very presence reminded her that being good was always better than being perfect. Being good would bring her the greatest success.

"I don't know how you two would survive without me," she told them. "And I don't know how I would survive without you."

This made Mrs. Shen smile. "So how's today going, Keisha?" she asked. "Better than yesterday?"

"Even better than today, in fact," Keisha said with a smile.

"I don't understand what that means," Mrs. Shen said. "But I like it."

And Keisha replied, "So do I."

Math went as smoothly as could be expected. Keisha answered questions about fractions and gave thumbs-ups to her classmates when they answered questions about fractions, even if they got them wrong.

At recess, the willow tree called to her once more, but she didn't sit down under it. Instead, she roamed the playground, helping more people. There weren't any other bags of Skittles to give out, but there were more smiles to go around. And the kids who were pretending to be superheroes got to witness what a real superhero was.

When art finally rolled around again, Keisha was thrilled to see that none of her classmates left the room to go to the Dungeon. They all worked on sculptures in clay.

Riley made a fish stick—don't worry, she didn't eat it.

Bryce made a gummy bear—worry, he considered eating it.

Carson made a clean shirt—always good to have a backup, even if you can't physically wear it.

Hunter made a butt—we are talking

about Hunter Barnes, after all.

And Keisha, of course, made a clock—so she would always remember this very, very long day.

Science was the only class left in the very, very long and memorable day. And this would be Keisha's first and only crack at it. So when Mrs. Shen announced, "Everyone take out your homework," Keisha acted on instinct.

Her instinct told her to be honest. "I'm afraid I didn't do it," she said.

"Keisha," Mrs. Shen replied, "that's so unlike you."

"Me too," Hunter announced, and he gave Keisha a nod to show her that they were in this together. "I didn't do my homework, either."

"Hunter," Mrs. Shen said, "that's so . . ."

"So what?" Hunter asked.

"I'm sorry to hear it."

Carson stood up next and nodded to Keisha exactly like Hunter had. "I didn't do it, either," he said.

And then Riley stood up and said the same thing.

Bryce, too.

Before long, more than half the class was standing, claiming they hadn't done their homework.

"This is highly unusual," Mrs. Shen said. "Was there a problem with it?"

The class was silent (especially the ones who were chewing Skittles), until Keisha spoke. "For me, it was a matter of time," she said.

Mrs. Shen nodded and smiled. "Fair enough. You can all hand it in tomorrow. And this is actually a good introduction to today's subject."

"People who don't do their homework?" Bryce asked.

"No," Mrs. Shen said. "I'm talking about time. What is time?"

Hunter pointed to the clock on the wall.

"A clock measures time, yes," Mrs. Shen said. "But it isn't actually time."

"Then what is time?" Keisha asked.

"Time is change," Mrs. Shen said. "If nothing in the universe changes, then there is no time, right?"

Keisha considered that for a moment. It was a difficult concept to get her head around, but it sounded right.

Time was change. And there was no doubt about it. Through the course of that very, very long day, things had changed. And Keisha had changed. Well, at least a little bit.

But for today, that was enough.

Chapter Thirty-Six
ON TIME

When the last bell rang and everyone was leaving for the bus, Keisha stopped Riley, Bryce, and Carson in the hall.

"Did you really not do your homework, too?" she asked.

They all looked at one another and shrugged. Then Riley said, "You helped us, so we helped you. It was a creative truth."

Keisha laughed and thanked them

multiple times over. Then she summoned her last bit of energy to run to the bus.

She was the first one to hop aboard, and she could choose any seat she wanted. She chose a hump seat, knowing that Hunter, who was often late for the afternoon bus, would probably have to sit with her.

As the other kids piled on, she pulled out the worksheet that was her science homework.

But just as she started to read the first question—

Thwap. Thwap. Thwap.

An orange-and-black butterfly bumped into her window, trying to escape the bus. So she opened the window, and a gust of air blew in. It grabbed the worksheet and lifted it.

But Keisha was too quick. She caught the worksheet before it could follow the butterfly out the window.

"Nice try, butterfly," Keisha said as it flapped away into the distance.

Chapter Thirty-Seven

COMING
NEXT . . .

Come back to Hopewell Elementary for another Locker 37 adventure, why don't you?

Will it involve cloning? Invisibility? A really ugly hat? Interdimensional fish sticks?

Only the locker knows for sure. So keep an eye out for more!